discard

טוביה שרוני

Little Dolphin's Big Leap

Story by Rebecca Johnson
Photos by Steve Parish

Solvay Elementary School
701 Woods Rd.
Solvay, NY 13209

GARETH STEVENS
GS
PUBLISHING
A Member of the WRC Media Family of Companies

Please visit our web site at: www.garethstevens.com
**For a free color catalog describing Gareth Stevens Publishing's list of high-quality books
and multimedia programs, call 1-800-542-2595 (USA) or 1-800-387-3178 (Canada).
Gareth Stevens Publishing's fax: (414) 332-3567.**

Library of Congress Cataloging-in-Publication Data

Johnson, Rebecca, 1966–
    [Dolphin's triumph]
    Little dolphin's big leap / story by Rebecca Johnson; photos by Steve Parish. — North American ed.
        p. cm. — (Animal storybooks)
    Summary: With practice, a young dolphin learns to leap out of the water like the adults do.
    ISBN 0-8368-5973-1 (lib. bdg.)
    1. Dolphins—Juvenile fiction. [1. Dolphins—Fiction.] I. Parish, Steve, ill. II. Title.
PZ10.3.J683Li 2005
[E]—dc22   2005042876

First published as *Dolphin's Triumph* in 2002 by Steve Parish Publishing Pty Ltd, Australia.
Text copyright © 2002 by Rebecca Johnson. Photos copyright © 2002 by Steve Parish Publishing.
Series concept by Steve Parish Publishing.

This U.S. edition first published in 2006 by
Gareth Stevens Publishing
A Member of the WRC Media Family of Companies
330 West Olive Street, Suite 100
Milwaukee, Wisconsin 53212 USA

This edition copyright © 2006 by Gareth Stevens, Inc.

Gareth Stevens series editor: Dorothy L. Gibbs
Gareth Stevens cover and title page designs: Dave Kowalski

Printed in the United States of America

1 2 3 4 5 6 7 8 9 09 08 07 06 05

Little dolphin loved to swim.

She loved to dive deep down
into the clear, blue water,

and she was always careful
to stay close to her mother's side.

Underwater, she could twirl and whirl and tumble and twist.

But, more than anything, she wanted to be able to leap into the air.

Every day, she watched the adult dolphins rocket through the water and leap toward the sky.

"Will I ever be able to do that?" she asked her mother.

"If you practice hard, you will," her mother replied.

Little dolphin practiced
every day. But, each time
she tried to leap into the air,
only her head came out
of the water.

Watching
from a distance,
her mother
said lovingly,
"What you need
is more speed."

"Let's swim down as deep as we can, and I will race you to the surface."

13

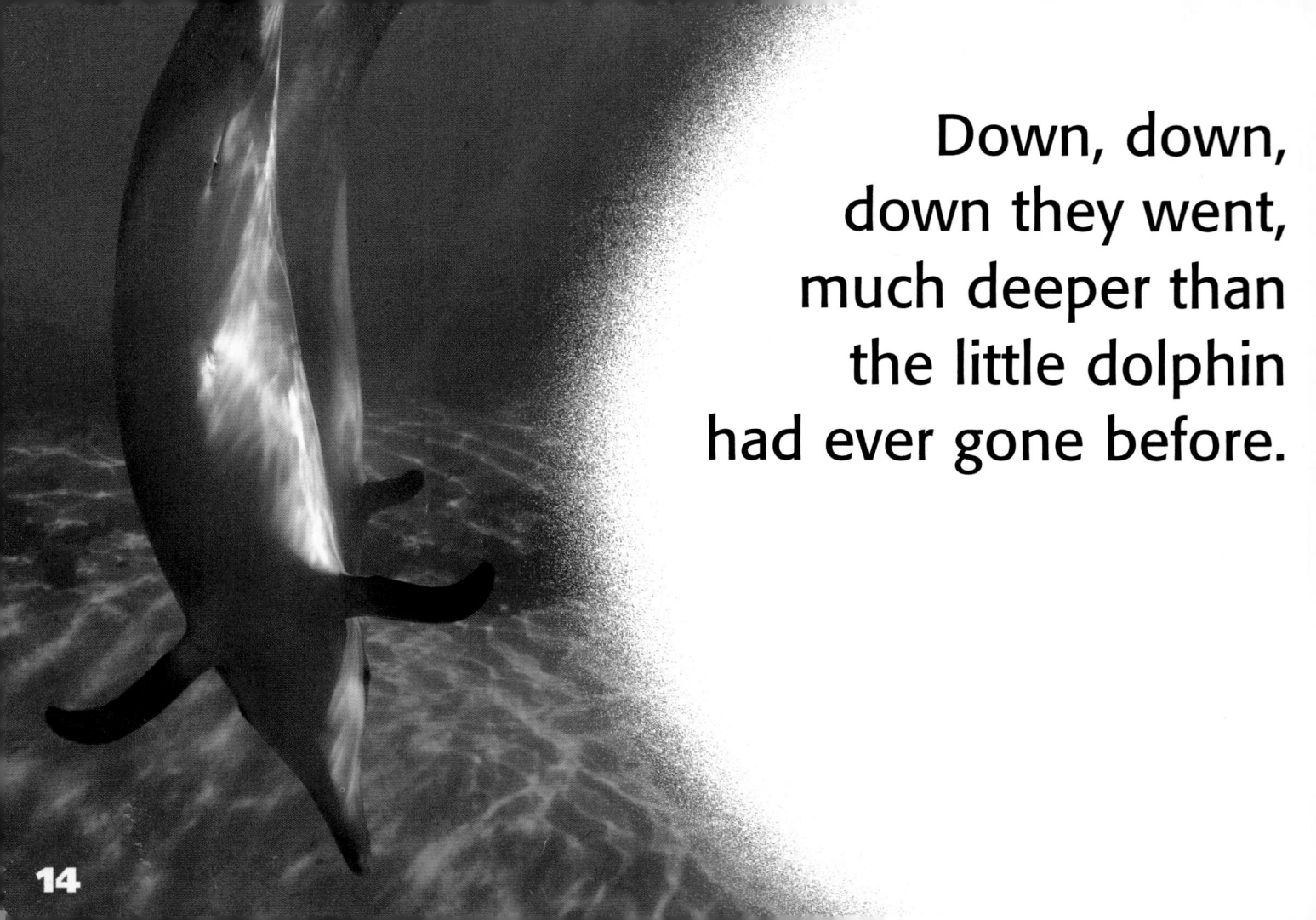

Down, down, down they went, much deeper than the little dolphin had ever gone before.

When they reached the seabed,
her mother said "ready . . . set . . . GO!"

Then, pumping
their tails with
all their might,
up, up, up
they swam.

"Keep going! Faster! Faster!" said her mother, and the little dolphin broke through the surface of the water like a torpedo.

Before she knew it,
little dolphin was flying
high through the air
in a beautiful arch.

18

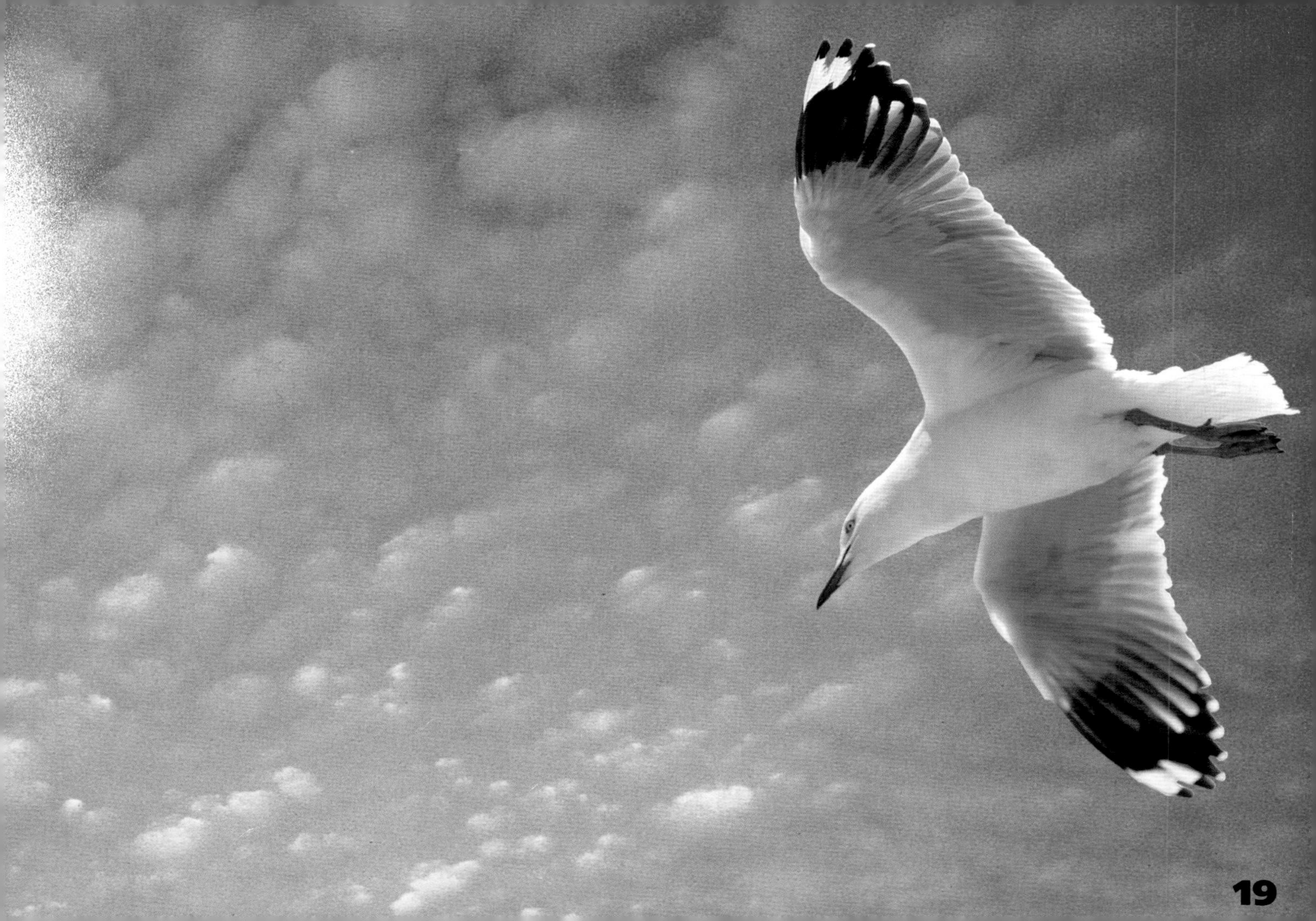

Then, she came diving down,
back into the sea.

Her mother squealed
with excitement.

"You did it!"
she cried.

Little dolphin
had done it, indeed.
And she was very happy!